Becky!

Other books by Pauly Hart

Supernatural Horror Novels
    By the Gates of the Garden of Eden
    The SRO (In progress)
Short Story Collections
    Sometimes I Write Tiny Stories
    Dreams Both Great and Small
    Adelphoi
Magazine
    Microzine: Volumes 1-5
Novellas and Novelettes
    Superior Respondent
    The Book of Lesser Voices
    Ouesso to Epena
    Mountain to Mountain
    Empire of the Dragon
    The Word of Yahweh unto Enoch

All books are available on Amazon.com and PaulyHart.com

Becky!

Pauly Hart

Published by Pauly Hart Art

Printed in the USA, where available.

ISBN: 9781955399371

Jacket and Cover Design by Pauly Hart

For information about the author, please visit PaulyHart.com

Library of Congress Catalog Data is available at: Loc.gov

This book is available on Amazon.com

For J...
Because you told me I shouldn't

I

Becky wasn't human. I mean, she had all the attributes of being human - smooth olive skin, perky B cups, and a smile that would make Colgate proud. But on the new moon she reset into something else. I mean literally it wasn't normal. And I don't know why but she always wanted me around when it happened. She would take off all her clothes in the complete darkness, usually in the open spot down in the forest behind my house. Oh, maybe that was it, that it was my house. So was I her spiritual protector or something? That would make some kind of weird sense. But whoops, here she goes again... It gets weird right about now. OK. So, she's standing full-on naked in the dark and like, has her arms out a little, but her fingers are grasping at the air I guess... I don't know. Then she starts scratching herself and it gets kinda terrifying now. I usually think about running away but I never do. Right now I'm halfway behind a tree peeking out in weird fascination.

Of course she knows I'm there. Becky isn't dumb. At this point she's super aware of everything around her. Her lungs huff and puff with the night air. It's September now and it's not really all that cold. This last January I brought an extra coat with me because she never wants to wear her old clothes that she's thrown off. I mean, sure, we wash them and then she'll wear them... But not ever after the weird night ceremony.

You probably want to know about her I guess.

OK, Becky moved here three years ago and we were besties immediately. Sure, she's a girl and sure sometimes we kiss in front of the other girls, but we're not lesbians. I mean, besides the times she has sex with me. Alright so maybe she's a lesbian. Well, no that's not true I guess. I guess Becky is bisexual because of that one time that French exchange student came with us. Serge. It was right before he had to go back to France and he came to the new moon thing she did. Becky had jumped him and ridden him like a bucking bronco. I'm sure he wasn't a virgin but he'd never had anything like that before. I kinda watched the whole thing, right there in the woods. Becky knew was watching, she looked at me most of the time she was on top of him. She sure has a thing for foreign exchange students. I'll tell you about another one in a while. Anyway.

At the ceremony… Ritual… Thing I was telling you about, she usually never tears her clothes but this time she does. She ripped her New Kids on the Block tee shirt and she'll be pissed when she remembers. "Bring back the time" is now torn right down the middle. Whoops. I don't like NKOTB but… Becky never had a normal sensibility on anything. Her normal khakis are alright, as usual. Dunno. Maybe she meant to tear that shirt? It was odd, but every month during her night thing, she came out of it a little different. Sometimes she would look at me like I was a new person… Or that maybe she was the new person? Like she didn't even *know* me, and the next day she interrogated me like she'd never met me before. She always tries to bite me like a vampire… Some things never change. Sometimes it's sex right off the bat. Not this time.

This time she's different. She's super different. I could tell it wasn't the normal Becky because of the really weird look in her eyes. Maybe it was her actual eyes? They hadn't changed color or anything but… Not a great way to tell in the dark. Oh - it was the way she looked at me alright. She was hungry. Um… Maybe hungry isn't the word, but she was more interested in me than normal. Like she'd just met New Kids for the first time. It was super awkward. Staring at my face, my boobs, everything.

So I'm helping her into my basement patio sliding glass door, the door that goes out to the deck by the hot tub and into the woods. Getting her dressed and getting her situated, all that stuff. It's around 10 pm and my parents know that we go out into the woods. "She loves stars" I tell them about Becky. Because Becky's parents always want her at my house during these times anyways. I think they know. They're super extra.

It means "extra weird" - Don't throw me shade. I don't talk like you... You'll just have to follow along.

She's actually hungry now so we go upstairs. My Dad is watching ESPN and yes everything is fine and mom is, well, mom is probably in the bathroom with the dildo. She thinks that no one knows but I know. I caught her one time and she offered to talk about it with me "anytime honey" but *GROSS* no thanks mom. And I think she knows about me and Becky but not everything obviously.

"Is it like being a werewolf?" I ask her as she's finishing leftover spaghetti in my room.

"What?" She looks up at me, sauce on her chin.

"Oh come on. The thing you do." I say.

"Oh. No." She says and grabs another bite of cold noodles with her fork... She seems like she really doesn't know how to use it. Like a little kid. But I wait for her to tell me and it's not too long before she does. You have to be patient with Becky and I'm super patient.

She gets a weird faraway look in her eyes. "It's like when you're born. Except you remember everything." She says a little thoughtfully, chewing slowly. "By the way, what is this stuff I'm eating? It's delic... Wait... Spaghetti? Is that right? Yes. This is good spaghetti." She says smiling, as if she'd won a prize.

Great, now she's being super stupid weird.

"How do you not know about spaghetti? You've eaten it a thousand times." I ask her.

"Oh simple child. I'm not the Becky you knew yesterday. Besides... The last thing I remember eating was roasted Reindeer before the Danes attacked our village."

II

If you ask me what happened that next week, I'd be in a hurry not to tell you but to skip right past it. But here I am, being asked, and so I suppose I'll let you know. Because I really think that I'm the only one alive to tell you the whole thing anyway. Well, OK I know I am. Whatever.

This... wasn't like other times. This was new. She was new. We spent the next two days skipping school. She must have asked me a zillion questions. We sat in the woods but mostly we went to the downtown library. She devoured the encyclopedia sets off the shelf, but wouldn't touch the public computers. "I'm not ready for Witchery" she says and goes back to Inventions that formed Modern Man volumes by one of those big publishing houses in the 1980's.

"Did you know about Nikola Tesla?" She's wide eyed and pawing at me. "We have to go see his machines!"

"What machines?" I dumbly ask.

"The great free electricity harnessers!" She declares loudly.

Several people look over at us and I tell her that I don't think they exist. This angers her and makes her a little sad. She goes back to reading until around three in the afternoon when the whole place is invaded by toddlers.

"Let us away from here." She says to me weirdly, and grabs my hand. We leave and walk into the sunshine. I'm assaulted by questions the rest of the afternoon. She asks to sleepover and we call her parents who are very understanding she says and fast forward to eleven at night when all of my house is asleep and she wants sex.

It happens and this time she's extremely violent and does things to me until I cry. I mean, I orgasm, but I cry too. I fell asleep with her holding me on the floor amidst blankets and pillows and bodily fluids and woke what felt like minutes later to her singing in the shower. It was already morning.

I have an en-suite bathroom and she was using it, door open, singing a very weird song I'd never heard before when my mom knocked on the door.

"Tiff! I've got breakfast downstairs on the island! I have to run! You girls taking bikes or walking to school?"

"Walking!" I yelled out from the floor.

"OK honey! Have a great day!" She called out.

"You too!' I called back.

The shower turned off and she came out. "Was that your mom?"

I rolled over and threw a pillow at her. "Yes. Why are you up so early?"

"It's a school day!" She said, naked. She looked at herself in the mirror. "Do you think the boys will think I'm pretty?"

I didn't know what to say. "Sure? I mean, they already do." I side eyed her. I think her breasts had gotten a bit bigger.

She turned left and right. Grabbing a towel off the bar, she wiped the mirror then continued to inspect herself.

"I think my breasts have grown," she said.

[Session Notes]

The man gets up from behind the desk and runs a hand through his hair. It's partially balding and it shows. He probably doesn't even know he's running his hand through his hair.

"That's along the right vein of what we're trying to get to. However, you claim that you feel she changed overnight. Tell me, do you believe it was maybe the onset of menstruation? That's been known to wreak havoc on all sorts of emotions."

"It wasn't a fucking period man. And we both went through that three years ago." I'm mad at him but try to calm down. "I know what periods are. We're not twelve."

He's standing at the little area in the office where there's a Kureg. He pops it open and puts in a Dunkin Donuts canister. It runs and the room suddenly has a distinct vanilla vibe. At least it wasn't pumpkin spice. Really can't stand that.

He gets his little handful of sugar and cream and walks back over to the desk.

"So. She really was a different person at each of these dark ceremonies she held?" He asks, settling back into the chair.

"No, not really. Maybe only a couple of times. But this time was the most obvious."

He blows on the coffee, not adding the cream or sugar, then takes a sip. He's one of those people who go '*aaahhh*' after a slurp and it's the most annoying thing ever.

"Alright." He said, after setting his coffee on the desk. "Let's talk about school."

"Sure." I said.

III

School was a hot mess, as it always was. She was wearing my clothes because we didn't go to her house for any new clothes. She had my "Spirited Away" T-shirt from Ghibli. It was my favorite shirt but she tied it in a knot in the middle so she could show off her bellybutton. Well, where a belly button should be anyway. She didn't have one. When I had first met her three years ago, she had told me that she was a test-tube baby. We hung out as much as we could that whole year and the summer after it. It was the end of 8th grade and we were going to High School after. The way our school system was, it was Kindergarten thru 8th and then High School was 9th - 12th. She said that she had already finished Primers before and so 8th would have been a repetition. "Except History" she had said. She already knew all of that.

And it was true. She got in trouble a couple of times because she argued with the teacher about the facts of what the teacher would say or what the textbook said.

"The whole thing is written from a Bankers cabal standpoint." She complained about the book to the history teacher. "There was nothing about slavery in the entire Confederate Rebellion. It was about economic freedom and the power to secede from the Union! Slavery was just a different way of life for the Southern States. Cheap labor drove the prices low! It was about Governmental control and the power of money distribution. Even Lincoln himself broke the

Constitution when he suspended the habeas corpus writ in 1861! You couldn't voice your opinion without being suspect of being a dissenter and guilty of treason!"

And off to the Principal's office she went. She won the argument but didn't make any friends with anyone. She only had me. She was almost placed in the AP classes across the board but her parents refused. They didn't want her to stand out too much. Basically she had me and her parents and that was all she said she really needed.

But her parents were super freaky though. Were they really her parents? She called them that, and they referred to her as "Our Becky" but I had my doubts. When we would go to her house, they would always act super funky. They didn't really do anything wrong, but there was never any actual parenting. Like they were her slaves or something. No advice, no discipline… Always bringing in snacks and asking if everything was "OK" - It was kind of sweet but also super creepy. What kind of adults did that? At supper they always prayed over their food, which I thought wasn't too weird… But the way they did it was super awkward. 'Great Father in flames grant us the pride to do this and that and whatever' is what they went on about but who prays like that? And they would always talk about the appearances she would show. No flashy clothes, no outspokenness, no this, no that. It was annoying that they were suppressing her.

"No, they're right." She would say. "I need to tone it down. I need to act like a normie. I've got big plans Tiff. Really big plans, and I don't want to fuck them up." She also wasn't allowed to cuss. "I mean, um, mess them up." She paused. "And I don't want you to mess them up either."

My parents adored her. I was their only child and most of my friends were books. They thought Becky had dropped down from heaven above to be my guardian angel and role model all at once. But seriously, what was important to me? There was nothing in all the world like lounging in my bean bag chair and reading a vampire romance novel with Double Stuffed Oreos and Orange Fanta. I mean, sure. Sometimes Pineapple Fanta, but gotta have my Double Stuffed. And that's all I really wanted until Becky would come climbing in my window and walk around the room fiddling with everything saying we should get out and do something. Then we would go and my parents were head over heels that I was getting out of the house and experiencing "the real world" as they called it. My parents had no idea about Becky. Not who she was, not what she was, and nobody, not even me, had any idea what Becky was capable of.

[Session Notes]

"Alright, so. I find this a little hard to believe. You had no other friends?"

"Does Karen Marie Moning count?" I asked.

He did a quick double-take at his notes. "Oh, um I don't think you've mentioned her. She's a classmate of yours?"

I laughed at him. "No idiot, she's an author."

He grimaced, put his pad down and stirred some more sugar into his coffee, side-eyeing me.

"I'm here to help you know. I'm not just listening for my benefit."

"I know, I know… I'm sorry." I said. And I really was. "That was when it all started to get funky."

"What do you mean?" He asked.

"That was the end of everything normal." I said.

"You describe any of her life normal?"

"No, no I mean, in comparison. After Kydra… It all…" I trailed off.

"After Kydra, what?" He said.

"Just shut up. Give me a second."

He waited patiently, looking out of the window until I was ready. Then I told him everything.

IV

After school we went to her house and brought Kydra over. She was an exchange student over from Africa. Agadez, Niger actually, though but she just told everyone Africa cause nobody at school knew where Niger was. Becky knew where it was alright. Becky even knew how to say hello in Hausa. "Sannu" she had said, and Kydra's was on her like shit on a stick. Kydra was super awesome at school and always wore some sort of pink outfit every day. We had gone over to Becky's house to study Algebra because there was a quiz tomorrow, and we all three hated it but Kydra was pretty good at it, so she said that we could study together. After that she would really have done anything Becky asked her. Well, she did. We didn't really study though, which I knew would end up happening.

Becky ordered us to take off our clothes and it was a really weird orgy. Becky told us what to do and we did it, like obedient slaves. It was awful and I hated it, but Becky could make me do things somehow. English was Kydra's fourth language, speaking French first, and Becky started telling her what to do in French. Becky was acting more and more off. Like, something was happening in her mind and she was making some seriously weird decisions.

She kept talking to Kydra in French. I had no idea what they were saying and I went along with it, because… Becky reasons. Then she said something.

"A frapper au visage." Becky said.

Kydra looked at her, eyes wide, like she didn't understand. Or maybe she did and that was the problem.

"I'll hold her." Becky said and went behind me, holding my arms back. "Do it," she said.

Huh?

I thought she was going to kiss me, but when she put her arm back and punched me in the mouth I shrieked.

I hit the floor and held my mouth with my hands. Kydra looked at me with pity.

"What the hell?!" I screamed at them both. My mouth tasted like blood and I started crying. What the hell was going on?

"Lui donner un coup de pied." Becky said.

Immediately, Kydra kicked me so hard I almost blacked out. She played soccer, so it really hurt.

I was crying and screaming for them to stop. Another kick, then Becky said something and Kydra jumped on top of me.

"Is everything alright?" Her mother was in the room suddenly. In front of her were three naked girls, brown, black, and white. The white one was on the floor, bleeding and crying while the black one with the pink ribbons in her hair beat her. Her daughter, the brown one, looked on and smirked.

"Sure mom. Everything's peachy." Becky said. Giving the "OK" sign with her fingers.

Kydra slowly stood up and looked down at her hands, not able to make eye contact with anyone. I curled up into a fetal position and didn't say anything, it was all whimpers.

For a long moment Becky's mom just looked at us and stared. She had this sort of plastic smile on her face, the kind you see a model wearing… You knew it was a facade.

"Well then…" She said, smiling and looking around. "You girls let me know when you want milk and cookies and I'll bring them up." Becky's mom said.

She walked backwards towards the door with that horrible smile on her face and closed the door behind her.

"Well." Becky said.

Kydra looked at me and then looked at her.

"I guess that's enough of that." Becky said.

I was done. I was so done. This was bullshit. We were supposed to be friends. What the actual fuck?.

"Wh-why?" I managed to wheeze out. It felt like one of my ribs was broken.

Kydra was huffing. I guess beating up people is a workout.

"This is what happens when people double-cross me." She looked down on me with disgust.

"Whe-when have I… Ever done that?" I managed.

"You haven't… Yet. And you never will, either. Will you?" She was an inch from my face. My lip had burst like a strawberry and blood poured from it.

N… No. No, I'd never do that. You're my friend. I just don't understand why you'd do… You'd do this!?"

"To keep you strong. To remember. You've seen me at my weakest. You of all people know. Now I'll show you what I am at my strongest. To know what I'm capable of. And what those who follow me will do for me." She said.

Then she leaned in and kissed me deeply. It was a mess of blood and spit. She rolled on top of me and ran her tongue all over my face and chest.

"Lui donner un orgasme." She told Kydra.

I didn't need to know French to figure that one out. And so, down on all fours they worked me over another way. I didn't need this. I needed new friends. Shit. I needed a hospital.

[Session Notes]

"That's… Wow… That's a lot to take in." The man said.

There was a long pause as he studied his notes.

"Were you and Becky intimate after this?"

No. Absolutely not. And she never included me in any more of it." I said.

"And were you and, uh, Kydra invol-"

"Absolutely not." I said, interrupting.

"And you've never told anyone about any of this, until right now?" He asked, taking another sip of coffee.

"No. You're the first. Because, maybe, you'll be the last."

V

I did go to the hospital soon after. Becky screamed and both parents had come rushing in the room in a panic. She told them I'd fallen off the balcony, even though I was right there on the floor. For God's sake, the mom acted like she hadn't seen anything before. It was surreal. I don't know if it was total mind control, like, some sort of hypnotism, but they bought it hook, line, and sinker. They carried me out to the car and drove me to the hospital and called my parents from there. In the car Becky had given everyone the story.

"No one remembers anything except that we were all studying. Got it?"

"Got it." Her parents said in unison from the front seat, both of them eyes forward.

She looked at Kydra who said: "Oui."

Then she looked at me and continued.

"...And then we went to the balcony and there was a bird that looked injured and stupid Tiffany wanted to save it but we told her not to. Kydra said - 'No don't!' but stupid Tiffany does anyway. She falls and hits her face on the first floor rail and then lands in a crumple. Got it? That's the story. Nothing else. No one remembers what kind of bird. Nothing. Just that."

But the doctors asked about my rib. I said I didn't know. They asked the parents, Becky, and Kydra. Same story. The doctors shrugged their shoulders and treated me. The police weren't called and we were alone until my mom showed up in tears.

"Ohmygod ohmygod ohmygod honeeeeeey!" She sobbed.

And then my dad got there in a panic. I'd never seen him so worried. Becky and family left, hugs and sobs all around. Seriously, everyone was crying. Becky put on the biggest show. But her parents said they needed to get Kydra home and soon it was just mom and dad and me. I had to stay in the hospital the night for observations and so the x-rays could come back. My mom decided to stay the night with me because my dad had a meeting in the morning, so he went home. Jerk. He could have stayed. I doubted he had a meeting. It was probably the Bears game. Whatever. *Sayonara dickhead.* But mom tucked herself in a little corner and used the extra blanket as I drifted off to la-la land.

The door shutting woke me up. Mom was still asleep and it wasn't a nurse. It was Becky.

This big stupid smile on her face told me it was still this new Becky. This new Becky that I didn't know. The one that liked to beat up her friend she's known for so many years. This new Becky that was a complete and utter asshole. Hello Asshole.

I must have said that outloud. She said hello back.

"You doing alright? I hear you'll be released in the morning. The nurse station told me. You aren't going to tell anyone about what you think happened are you? About any of it? You're going to stick to the story right? The story of what actually happened? How you fell?"

There was an inference that was deep in that little spiel. One that said: *'And if you don't, you don't want to know what will happen to you.'*

God I knew what would happen if I said anything else. Anything. Even about the bird. And about the rib. Somehow she knew they'd ask. I would agree.

"Just say you don't know. It's all a blur. You reached out, you fell. That's all. Nothing more." Her eyes were dead set on mine, not wavering. Trying to control me. It was working.

"Sure Becky. Whatever you say." I said.

"Whatever I say?" Her tone changed immediately. She sat down on the side of the bed and put her hand on mine. I cringed but didn't move it. "But honey," she continued, "we all know that you're a bit clumsy and that, well, these things just happen to you from time to time. And we never know when you'll have your next incident. We just... Never... Know..." And her hand on mine was a vise.

I knew when my next incident would be. Never. That's when.

I was going to have to kill this bitch.

[Session Notes]

"I gotta skip ahead a little here," I told the man.

"How far ahead?" He asked, tapping his pencil on the little pad he had been taking notes on.

"Maybe until the end of the year. Summer break. Because it was at the beginning of Summer when everything went down."

"Went down? You mean the murders? He asked.

"Well. I mean everything." I said.

"Everything." He repeated.

"Everything." I insisted.

"Alright. But can you fill in a little of the missing pieces between the two times. There's not much we don't know about the time 'it all went down' as you said, but how did s-"

"*LISTEN*." I don't want to tell you *everything*, OK? At least not right now. But I'll give you enough to fit the first part with the end." I said, insisting.

He put his hands up. "Fine. Fine. Have it your way. We'll revisit this later. Tell me what you want to tell me."

VI

It was summer. Well, OK, it was three days before the end of school and it was a new moon. Becky and the seven were walk… Oh yeah, there were seven of us by then. Kydra and five others and me. And they all acted like Kydra. They did everything she asked, like brain-washed Nazis or something. Her homework, her liquor runs, everything. Well I suppose her parents gave her all the alcohol she needed so that wasn't really a thing but she'd get the girls to steal it anyway. Sometimes they got caught but they always got off with a warning because all of the girls were the most popular and smartest in school. Becky made them drop out of whatever sports they were doing just so she could tell them what to do.

See, right after the accident I stayed out of school for three weeks and Becky was busy. Then, the night I'm supposed to come back to school, she and these six other girls come over and give me a makeover and then ta-ta, we'll see you tomorrow. Becky had been coming by every day after school with my homework and I hadn't thought anything about Kydra or anyone else for that matter… But when "The Horde" showed up for the makeover, it freaked my parents out a little, and me a whole lot.

At school they called me 'Birdie' instead of Tiffany. Everyone did. Becky announced it, so everyone did it. Like, the whole school. Even the teachers. When I got back to Biology, Mrs. Shea says: "Welcome back Tiffany… I mean, Birdie." It was humiliating at first, but then, it was almost like the coolest nickname ever. I knew what Becky was doing. She was never going to let me forget what happened. It worked. My new nickname was almost a new identity within her group. So I towed the line and fell in to do whatever the others were doing.

There was some bad stuff we did. Like, legit evil. I don't think anyone at the Frat house will say anything, but there was one night were we basically did every guy in the place. They tied Kydra down and had every guy in a line on her… Anyway. There was a lot of bad stuff happening all night… No, don't look at me like that, I won't tell you the name of the Fraternity, but I'll tell you about something else.

Mr. Windly didn't like Becky. He was a hard-core Jewish Christian guy who taught History and Government. No I don't know how that works and I don't care. We lit his car on fire. It was at his house. One of the girls who worked as an assistant during study hall in the front office found his address. In his driveway was his gross mustard Thunderbird and we lit it up.

Becky was pretty smart about it. She had Kydra get into the car, pop the trunk, and then Becky put in some hardware stuff. I don't know, it was like chemicals. Some brake fluid and some pool supplies, and some other stuff. We set it up, closed the trunk and drove down the block and waited. Within minutes there was a huge *whoosh* and the car was on fire. We were far enough down the block that we could see it light up the whole house and the neighbors. There was a lot of chemicals. The thing was an inferno. We almost hit a white Honda Civic as we drove away but nobody ever found out it was us.

Anyway, that's one of the worst things. Uh, we caused a flood in the bathroom at H.H. Gregg. We stole a whole cash register from Aéropostale, Set the sprinkler system off at the mall... Just lots of trouble. Lots more stuff I'm not even going to tell you about. So much you wouldn't even believe me.

Oh don't give me that look. OK I'll tell you another one you won't think is true. You know that Alpine Audio shop over on Kellogg? Ok well Lydia steals her dad's work truck and we go over there, cut a hole in the back of the shop, and walk out thousands of dollars' worth of amps and speakers. Look it up. They never found out who did it. It was Becky and... Lydia and Kydra and everyone else. Me I suppose.

Somehow Becky crawled into my mother's mind and she became *one of them*. And I think you know what I mean when I say it like that. Like, everything Becky does is good and nothing she would ever do would lead anyone to harm. That kind of person. The hypnotized kind. And wow, whenever my dad and her would argue you would think he was trying to bad mouth Jesus himself by the way she talked about how good Becky was for me. It was unreal. I basically could do whatever I wanted, and so could the rest of The Horde, now that Becky had infected all of their minds. Becky ruled the school and the town.

Kydra was going to have to go home after the school year was over so Becky set up a meeting with her Stateside parents and her real parents on the phone at the School Counselors' office. I don't know why I was invited but I was there too, I guess to lend moral support. Everyone agreed that staying in the States would be in Kydra's best interests so she would stay on here another year. It worked out for Becky.

But not really. I mean… Did it work out that she showed her one weakness by inviting me for moral support? Becky didn't need any. But it got me thinking about my relationship to her. I mean, why was I always around? Why had I been the first person she attached herself to? Why was I the only one who needed to be "taught a lesson?" And why couldn't she hypnotize me.

And I started asking myself: Was she afraid of me? But why? What kind of power did I hold over her? Was I some kind of horcrux like Harry Potter's scar? Was she Voldemort? That idea was super dumb but it was the closest working theory that I had so I decided to test it at the party.

The famous O'Dooly party.

[Session Notes]

He stood and stretched when I came to a stop in the story.

"You want a snicker bar?" He asked. "I'm getting one."

Do they have Double Stuffed Oreos?" I asked.

He thought about that. "No, just regular."

"I'll take regular Oreos then I guess."

"Be right back." He said, and walked out.

I looked around. Regular office. Nothing special. He was a neat guy, very orderly. He had all his ducks in a row. I'm not even kidding. Tiny mallards were arranged in a single file line on the desk facing left. It was kinda cute but also kinda sad. I picked one up, looked at it and hurriedly put it back down when I heard the door open.

Walking in, he had an Orange Fanta and Oreos for me. He was alright after all.

"Really want to ask about her breasts but that seems like a weird question." He said as he sat down. He had a Cream Soda flavored Doctor Pepper and *snickt* the top open then unwrapped his Snickers.

"Yuuuup." I agreed. "Total creeper."

He laughed and shrugged his shoulders. "Well, were they actually bigger? Was she going through that stage?"

"Kinda weird because she never really stopped developing. She looks like she has the body of an old lady. Like a 25 year old." I said though a mouthful of Oreos.

He laughed. "Your what, 18?"

"Yeah, so?"

"Old isn't 25, is my point."

"Well then, a fully matured woman." I said.

"That's the one." He agreed.

He gazed at the ceiling "I have another weird question…" He hesitated.

"OK."

"The lesbianism aspect…" He began.

"You mean when she raped me?" I asked.

"Yeah." He said, apologetically.

"Didn't happen again with me, but it did with the other girls. I was never invited. But I heard stories that really made me want to die."

"I see." He said.

I really doubt he did.

VII

I gotta tell you something important. Well I think it's important. It's about my theory about being a horcrux and how I was attached to Becky. Well Becky didn't know it because we didn't have all of our classes together, but I talked to Mr. Windly about his car. I didn't admit anything but I did ask him about some things as well, and spiritual stuff too. Like, wow, he went into this thing about fallen angels and demons and something called watchers, and hoo-boy it was out there. But something he said made a lot of sense based on what I thought Becky was becoming or had become. She had only mentioned it a couple of times about her previous weird life... Like, and I was thinking that she had just been talking about like, her life back in Europe. I mean, I supposed it was Europe or Northern Europe because of that thing about eating reindeer.

But besides that first night I totally never got any information out of her. I would ask but she'd dismiss the question and talk about something else, and I never pushed. And you know the strange part really? She hadn't once invited me to her night ceremony thing.

"I don't do that any more," was all I got out of her.

I mean, I never asked her if she was a time traveler or an interdimensional alien but you know, when Mr. Windly started talking about nephilim demons, the hairs on the back of my neck stood on end. You know, when you get goose pimples? Anyway, it happened then. When he said that the cast out souls of the watchers were bound at the foundations of the earth for a thousand years but then one day they'd be released to create chaos on mankind. That was what really got me. Like. Woah. Maybe Becky was a fallen angel. Or at least the thing was that was inside of her.

But why was I important? I had to find out. I had to get rid of her.

The test I had planned was pretty elaborate but simple all at once. All of the planning was in my mind so there was never anything written down anywhere. She would have found that and probably kill me. So I made this, what do you call it? A decision tree? Fuzzy logic path? Something like that. You probably already know what it is. If she says this thing, I do that thing. But it's like outthinking Becky. She probably lies awake at night and makes decision trees in her mind about everything, like some sort of evil chess grandmaster. She always has a plan. Like Tyler Dyrden from Fight Club. Always doing something and the main guy, whatever his name was, never knows anything. Oh but I'm not Becky, if that's what your thinking, cause that's just a stupid solution. No. Becky is a demon and I had to fucking kill her. I mean, you've seen her actual body.

So we're at the party and things are hopping, and there's no obvious decision tree split so I'm just hanging loose drinking a beer. There was a lot of beer at the O'Doolys. And you're probably thinking - yeah great joke. O'Douls at the O'Doolys. But nope. It was Coors or something. I don't know, I'm not really a beer drinker. It could have been Miller High Life or something. Whatever, we were just hanging out and Becky says let's all go outside and I leap at the opportunity. This is it. It might seem small in every other social circle but this was the gamble of a lifetime in mine.

"Why don't we all go upstairs and check on the rooms and see who's having sex?" I say, acting a little drunk. I'm a lightweight but I was still all there upstairs. Not even a body buzz yet. But see, this was the test. This was *THE TEST*. It was super obvious because I made it so, but I wasn't disobeying her, I simply offered (what I figured was) a cooler suggestion. And all the girls ate it up.

"Hell yeah." They all said, and didn't even look Becky's way. And that was it. I had won. There really hadn't even been a battle. I didn't disobey anything she had said, I had simply ignored her and given everyone a better opportunity.

[Session Notes]

"Sorry, but what does this have to do with the murders?" He asked getting up.

"Nothing. It all leads up to that."

"But in the police report you're nowhere on the scene."

"I know." I said. "After I killed Becky, I left."

"The police ruled it a suicide. She shot herself and drowned in the pool." He said, sitting back down.

"Because I told her to." I said.

He paused for a minute. He leaned forward and adjusted the duck I had picked up. He smiled, leaned back in his seat and put his fingers on his temples.

"Tiffany... When you came to us, you told us you had information leading to the arrest of suspects that were the cause of the deaths at the party."

"Yes! Because Becky killed them! And then I killed her!" Problem. Solution. Simple." I stood and put my hands on his desk. "Because she was a demon in a human body! Her parents were Demon worshippers! Pagan temple serfs of the Council of High Ifrit Djamotoroth! Fucking look it up!"

He put his hands in the air. "Now let's just calm down. Everything is going to be fine. Have a seat why don't you?" He waved his hand to the chair I had just lept from.

I signed in exhaustion. How could I relax now? "Tell you what. Can I just explain to you my part and let you fill in the rest?"

Smiling, he said: "Sure," folded his hands over his chest and let me continue.

VIII

So we went upstairs to check out the fuck-pads. My one-time command over the group hadn't messed with her. She acted like nothing had happened but went upstairs last, right behind me.

"Never again." she whispered to me, and then pushed forward through the group, same plastic smile on her face. My whole body shuddered like I had just escaped death

Not much was happening upstairs so we kinda went through drawers looking for maybe, I don't know, loose change, or jewelry. The O'Doolys were pretty loaded. Not like super rich like balls dragging on the street or however Macklemore says it… But rich. We didn't find any jewelry or anything, but in one of the rooms there was a gun safe and the password was on a post-it on the laptop. 4-3-3-1. Becky had one of the girls punch it in and it clicked. Kydra opened it up and there were three handguns inside. One of them was a really old silver gun. The one with the spinning barrel. Revolver, yeah. It was in this red velvet case with six silver bullets. Becky got this really crazy look in her eyes and told Kydra to pick it up and load it.

Bro. It was legit serious. Kydra passed it around and we all got to hold it. Yeah I've thought it about it a lot but Becky never touched it. Probably smart enough with fingerprints and everything. I think that's part of her criminal mind, she actually never touched anything that could be brought back to her in any of the things we did. Anyway. So someone hands the gun to me and I flash a quick look at Becky and for a millisecond I see fear in her eyes but I hand it to one of the other girls and don't look at her again.

"Bring it downstairs," she says.

So we do this really elaborate game of Russian Roulette except it's Kydra holding the gun in the middle of the living room with Becky standing on the fireplace mantle asking questions. Kydra closes her eyes and spins around and then Becky says stop and whoever it's pointing at has to answer whatever question Becky asks. Robert Brownlee apparently molested his younger brother when he was nine. Axel Goodtenrod masturbates to gay porn, but they have to be black men. Heather Transom steals lipstick from Walgreens. And I think that the best one is that Jeremy Lanthrap once streaked through the College game with a rubber horse-head on. Everyone thought that was hilarious because we all knew about the streaking but no one knew who had done it.

So then Becky has Kydra spin around and she screams: "Stop!" And it lands on me.

And she doesn't ask me anything like my most hideous crime or darkest secret or anything. She simply cocks her head and asks: "Birdie, do you love me?"

And I say: "No" without hesitation.

And the crowd is silent.

"You fucking what?" Becky says and her face contorts into this hideous sculpture of what her face used to look like, except it's not her face but a rearranged version of her face, contorted in anger.

Everyone sees her face. It's like it's melting or something. And Kydra sees it and the gun falls from her hand and hits the floor and it goes off. Oh yeah it was loaded. With all six bullets. Except now that there were now suddenly and explosively only five bullets in the gun, the whole place turned into an instant madhouse.

Then I ran away. I ran as fast as I could. I knocked over a pretty girl with blonde pig-tails and I knocked over two of the guys from track and field. I was possessed.

And that's all I know.

[Session Notes]

"So you didn't really kill Becky." He said, leaning back.

"No. I lied."

"And you didn't tell her to kill herself."

"No. I lied again." I said.

"How much more of it is lies?" He asked.

"Oh not much more. Or maybe none of it. Or all of it."

"Which one?" he asked.

"Well, I may have exaggerated about a couple of things but, no actual lies. Maybe. Or maybe I did kill her, Maybe I grabbed the gun from Kydra and shot her." I said, sarcastically.

He closed his eyes. "Tiffany, would you ple…"

"Or maybe I told Kydra to kill her." I said, interrupting.

"Would you please…"

I laughed out loud leaning forward and grabbed the desk.

"No! No wait! I had her grab the gun and had her shoot herself!" I screamed, crying so hard from laughter. I threw myself back in the chair and had a good one out of that. I laughed so hard my sides hurt.

He stood up and ran his hand through his hair and walked around the desk. "You know, her parents have disappeared."

"The Satanists?"

"I thought they were something else. Something about an Ifrit."

"Yeah, samesies." I said.

"But there's a lot that you've got right. Her physical description. No belly button. No real history, and surprisingly, not a single fingerprint of her because she doesn't actually have any."

"What?" I asked.

"Adermatogliphia: The lack of fingerprints on fingers." He said, reading it from his little pad.

"Wild." I said. "I guess I'd never looked."

"Most rare indeed." He said.

"So that's it?" I asked. "Are you going to arrest me now or what?"

"Nope. Thanks for coming in." He said, shaking my hand. "You're not a suspect. And we have as many versions of the story as we do witnesses to the shooting. Six people dead. Either all forty-eight of you did it or what most people say is true."

That stopped me. "Wait. I didn't know anyone else died."

"Oh yes Tiffany. Five of the shots were exact to the point of a marksman and the sixth one was a point blank shot. That's the story everyone gives. Becky's body was found in the pool, her face completely disintegrated." He stated matter of factly.

"The sixth one…" I started

"Becky shot herself." He said simply.

"But that's it? You're really not concerned with all the shit I talked about? My rape? That guy molesting his brother?

You don't care? It's just - Oops another teenage gun rampage and that's it?"

"Do you want us to pursue any of it? Do any of the parents want to? Do we want to dig and dig until all of the people at the party relive the moments on a daily basis or do we want to move on? Do you want to move on Tiffany? Do you just want to go to college and forget about it... Live a normal life?"

I said nothing, taking it all in.

He got up and walked behind me, pacing the room while I thought. "I'm just a special consultant with the FBI Victim Assistance Program. But I can pass it along if you really want me to. I doubt anyone wants to pursue any of those leads. I'm sure that the teens and the parents of the deceased will have enough now that the funerals are finally over, the Facebook memories written, and everyone moves away and goes to their new school."

I paused.

"People move on Tiffany. And I understand how this affects you more than it affects anyone else... But let me ask you a question," he said. "Have you had counseling about any of this? Do your parents know about any of this? I mean, the weird stuff? Am I seriously the only one you've talked to?"

I smiled. "My parents have absolutely no clue about anything else. I went to a party and Becky shot 5 people and then killed herself. That's what everyone believes and that's what the news said, and so that's evidently what you think too. So why the fuck do I need to tell anyone? And why haven't I told anyone before? I had to tell someone... And I only wanted to tell it once. You're the guy. You do what you want with the information."

He nodded. "And your mom?"

"What about her?" I asked.

"How does she feel about it all?"

"Oh she still cries all the time about her beloved second daughter." I said.

"That's got to be rough." He said.

"You have no idea." I said, and walked out the door.

[Postscript]

A small click in the ceiling and a tinny voice crackles. "Give us a minute until we ensure she's left the building," a European voice said.

The man walked over to the Kureg and selected a Starbucks cup, put it in and pushed the button. He put in cream and sugar and sat down. After a few minutes a small door opened to the left of his bookshelf. It didn't look like a door, just a paneled part of the wall. A small man in a bad suit walked in. His black beard was oiled and he wore gold rimmed glasses, the lenses tinted a rosy color.

"Becky put the gun up to her nose and pulled the trigger." The small man said.

"Not the most effective way to shoot yourself, and I've never heard of anyone doing it like that before but it completely disintegrated her face." The man in the chair said. "And that's the good thing. No one can identify her." He smiled. "Oh and get this! We've looked everywhere and do you know what we found? Not a single photo of her anywhere."

"Mmm…" The small man hummed thoughtfully. "She was good." Where do you think they got the body double?"

The man in the chair laughed. "That was actually me. I had a runaway in Delaware I used. It was a one man job. I did the move and the stage. Got a rape and a sacrifice out of it though."

The small man glowered at him.

"What? I used a biohazard suit and a condom. No DNA. But it was so messy though. Ruined a good pair of gloves." The man in the chair said.

"Very Dexter Morgan, but very foolish. Next time when you have a task, be single focused." He stood still for a long time contemplating. "When do you think Becky will emerge?" The small man asked.

"Unknown. The high priest says it depends on Birdie's cognitive dissonance. We know she's the strongest one to have ever been picked... But we don't know when the possession will fully take. Becky might push through when she's twenty five. Hopefully by then. We have operation 2050 to look forward to." The man in the chair said, getting up.

He straightened his sports coat and stood with the smaller man who was by the window. They could just see Birdie's car leaving the parking lot. A white Honda Civic also left the parking lot, seemingly at random.

"Good agent?" The man asked.

The small man answered. "The same one we've been using this whole time. Did you ever see them?"

The man raised his eyebrows. "No. I don't think I ever did."

The small man smiled. "Good agent."

The intercom buzzed and announced: "Call on line two."

The man looked at the smaller man and patted him on the shoulder. "Get some coffee Sergei. Take a break. We've got a couple of years to wait."

"I'll go home instead. I've got to feed my guests." The small man smiled.

"Oh? I didn't know you still had tenets in the basement."

"Just three." The small man smiled wickedly.

"Until then." The man said. "All hail our Lord in flames." and gave a salute.

The small man also saluted. "All hail our Lord in flames."

www.ingramcontent.com/pod-product-compliance
Lightning Source LLC
Chambersburg PA
CBHW021005150626
46549CB00012BA/1310